Lovely Day and Other Stories

Femdom Mind Control

Flash Fiction – Vol. 11

S.B.

Table of Contents

◎ A Long Ride - 7
◎ Horny - 9
◎ How to Sell an Illusion - 14
◎ Lesson Number One - 19
◎ Lesson Number Two - 22
◎ Lovely Day - 25
◎ Old New - 27
◎ Slavery Night - 33
◎ The Horror of Brunwyn - 38
◎ The Pet's Reward - 44
◎ You Never… - 46
◎ Vampires - 47

Every day is a good day to lose your mind.

A special thank you to all patrons of

Spell... B-O-U-N-D.

A Long Ride

"When we met, did you ever think we would end up like this?"

It was an overplayed question, a cliché Luke had heard so many times before, yet the more she said it the more he loved the repetition game. Mandy smiled and the cute little freckles on her cheeks smiled too as her voice faded into a whisper to go for another round.

"When we met…" she continued at a slower pace. "…did you ever think…" her slanted green eyes looked down at him. "… we would end up like this?"

"Yes… and no," he thought or, at least, he thought he thought… God, thinking about thinking is hard when you're not used to thinking at all! A lock of rose gold hair massaged the back of his neck.

"When we met…" he panted, warm creamy liquid dripping from his lips. "I thought… we would end up in bed together sooner or later but not that I…"

"… would suck a big black rubber cock instead?" She giggled. "It's funny how things work out, isn't it?"

"I am under your control..." Luke justified himself, aching tongue in perfect sync with his engorged lips.

"You certainly are," she thrusted the phallus deep inside his throat. "but the sixty-four-million-dollar-question is…"

“When… mffff… am I… mfff… not?”

“Not only you know all the answers but all the questions, too,” Mandy concluded. “Just the way I like it… Three, two, one… wake up.”

Luke blinked, his once distant visage becoming focused again. The sound of angry horns all around reminded him he was still stuck in traffic next to his twin sister, the hypnodomme. The gear stick of the *Land Rover Freelander* they were in was covered in slob.

“Did I…?” he tried to ask.

“Of course not.” Mandy lied, wondering if her new shade of purple lipstick would look good on him next time.

It was going to be a long ride to their mother’s house.

Horny

Ashley unwrapped the mystery box that had just been delivered at her annual Halloween party, puzzled as to why she was the recipient of something she clearly hadn't ordered. Her best friend Sylvia peeked above her shoulder from atop her cowgirl boots, curious. She spoke first:

"Boy, the delivery guy sure disappeared in a heartbeat! It's a shame though as he was cute. So… what is that?"

"I haven't got a clue. I never even heard of this store before..." Ashley responded as her fingernails caressed the smooth inside and unveiled… "Oh!"

"Cool, a pair of horns!" Sylvia exclaimed with glee. "You know what? I think those will look super with the rest of your outfit!"

She couldn't help but laugh. Ashley held the pair of dark red horns up high and a sexually charged laugh escaped her lips. They were incredibly arousing to the touch.

"Huh? I'm dressed as Red Riding Hood, silly! And she is sweet and innocent, and… okay, this thing is sure made of a strange material! Here, touch it and tell me what you're feeling."

Sylvia rubbed one of her hands in them, absorbing a mystical energy into her skin. As a mere mortal, she wasn't supposed to understand it but could enjoy its flow and declare: "Wow! They give off a tingling warmth that's quite intoxicating!"

"I know! Why do you think that is?"

"Who cares? Sweetie, you should try them on! I would do it myself but there's not a single ounce of red in my costume at all. So what if Red Riding Hood was a spotless soul in the fairy-tale? This is Halloween, and the fun lies in twisting traditions. Go on, let me see how they look on you!"

"Okay, I'll try them," Ashley agreed as she brought the hood to her back, the mesh of silky, black curls shining in its entire splendor. "They don't seem to have anything to make them stick so I wonder if…"

Instantly, they merged with the wavy hair, their tips extending forward like they were real horns and not just a pretty decoration.

It was then that, from the ruckus of the actual party taking place past the main corridor where both women stood, along came an impersonation of Tarzan (or was it George of the Jungle?), swinging his arms and spilling fruit punch all over the floor.

Brad was his name, party-crashing his vocation, a neighbor who always drank too much, and enjoyed spoiling everyone's fun at every possible opportunity. It was impossible to now how much he had already drunk, but it was more than enough to make him a real nuisance.

"Now, that's something to raise a man's pole way up in the air! If Red Riding Hood is horny, then here I am, baby!" he spurted, a thread of white spit accumulating in the upper-corner of his lips.

Ashley looked at him enraged as the unnatural energy emanating from the horns increased in intensity. Something was changing in her ways of thought; power grew from the inside and outside of her outfit and now that very repulsive creature that believed to be a man was being seen through half-angelic, half-demonic eyes.

Sylvia couldn't help but notice the gradual modification in posture and the bewitching cadence of her friend's fingers as tiny sparks of emerald green ran through them. At the same time, the Red Riding Hood outfit was becoming tighter, assuming the same dark, seductive color and tactile sensation of the pair of horns. She whispered in her ear: "Ashley, what's happening?"

"I'm being elevated…" the brunette retorted, her voice chilly and hot, mellifluous and irresistible. "Now, watch as I teach him a lesson he should have learned a long time ago."

The new Ashley glided across the corridor stopping right in the front of the drunk guest and purring: "Do you think you're man enough for me?"

"Are you serious?" Brad asked, amused. "Ashley, I'm the real king of the jungle and what I got beneath my thong can keep you pleased for eternity and a day!"

Her eyes glowed green for a fraction of a second.

"Then why can't I see a thing? It would be nice if you had hard balls and a throbbing dick, but you don't," she smirked. "At least, not anymore…"

"Huh? What's going on in your sick…?" Brad looked down, at the smooth skin in its crotch area, a perfect clearing. It had no protuberances, no sex traits, nothing! "What?!! What did you… how did you… my dick and balls! You took away my dick and balls!"

"Yes, I did, and this is where you go down at my feet in utmost devotion, say 'Thank you so much!' and then… Get the hell out of my house and party!"

"Keep dreaming, you…" but as the words of malice came out, his body and mind crumbled under the weight of her order and he knelt. Blank, he droned: "Thank you so much…" before getting up and going away into the dead of night, a Halloween slave.

Sylvia covered her mouth with her left hand in shock, terror even. Strings of rationalizations collapsed inside her mind. Ashley was no longer human. In her shadow, a heart-shaped tail slithered around her waist.

"There was only one thing that jerk was right about…" the domineering woman confessed whilst looking into the perplexed eyes of the one who had been her best friend. "I am feeling horny right now and there are many inside this house whom I wish to have servicing my needs… You're the first in a long list, Sylvia and I'm sure you'll do a wonderful job at it, my little slutty cowgirl!" a finger pointed to the floor. "It's your turn to kneel."

She obeyed and then crawled behind her owner as she moved to reclaim her place as Queen of the party.

How to Sell an Illusion

The Zenobia Diamond: a more than 100 karats beauty like no other, sporting the top color ranking of Fancy Vivid Yellow. It was unearthed somewhere in South Africa a couple of years ago, and it's a rare treat for the eyes of many, an otherworldly desire for avid collectors, and the dream of any prestigious jewel thief.

Take Dean Mason, for example, a.k.a. The Swift God, and one of the best in his field of expertise. For a long, long time, he had dreamed of the day when he would be able to take that preciousness as his own. Well, at least for a short period of time seeing he was a mercenary for hire and stole anything for anyone who had enough money to burn.

Learning every single detail of the tight security system devised for that particular exhibit had been a laborious and meticulous process but, eventually, he had found a way to bypass it all: heat sensors, infrared arrays, pressure plates, invisible lasers, the works, until he had finally opened the crystal case without triggering the dozen of silent alarms surrounding it. This was his moment of glory, the peak of thieving grandiosity... he would always be remembered as the one who had managed to swipe...

... a giant onion?!!

"What the fuck?" He thought as he looked at he was holding. He had come for a precious stone and got a bulb vegetable, instead? That made absolutely no sense! What made things worse was the fact that, once inside the display, He could see the perfectly cut diamond once again, tantalizing his senses with the promises of an incomparable wealth.

So where did the trick come from? Was it some sort of projection device He couldn't see? As much as he would love to figure out, the truth is time was running out and most certainly, the Museum Security, as well as the Metropolitan Police, were already on their way to arrest him.

He was about ready to leave when a silky woman's voice whispered behind her.

"Why the rush, Swift God? The exhibit wasn't to your liking?"

Dean turned his head to face her, a short-haired brunette wearing a masculine white suit that contrasted with his dark, clingy outfit. Her smile would have been a captivating one if it weren't for a single good tooth sparkling in the center of her mouth.

"Don't worry about security. No one is coming to disturb us at least for a couple of hours..." She added.

"And you are....?"

"Britney Caldwell, the top gun in charge of protecting what you came to stole. You look disappointed. What's the matter? You don't like onions?"

"Not really. I don't like your lack of sense of humor either. What's the angle, here?"

"Well, first of all, I wanted to show you I know how to sell an illusion. Secondly, I wanted to meet the man who will be blamed for the disappearance of the Zenobia once I run away with the real thing.... "

"Excuse me?!!"

Caldwell took two steps towards him and it was the first time he noticed the small, cylinder-like object in her left hand.

"Don't look so shocked! You're not the only thief in the business! I could have taken the gem a long time ago, but I needed the perfect scapegoat for the heist, preferably one that's currently being paid by my client's... competition!"

"Oh, so that's the game we're playing, huh?" He smirked. "Cute, but I'm not interested in taking the fall for something I clearly won't have the chance of doing in the first place."

"I knew you were going to say something like that which is why I brought this baby with me." She threw her the object he was carrying and watched him scramble to grab it before it crashed on of the pressure plates on the floor. "Do you know what it is?"

A quick examination gave him the right answer. "A case for a hypodermic needle. There's a switch here that triggers it but..."

16

"That's right, the contents of the syringe are empty. Onions usually make us cry, others have a nasty tendency of drugging us, even if we're wearing protective gloves..."

Dean started to feel dizzy almost immediately, his strength disappearing by the second. Caldwell moved in to grab him before he collapsed against the case and gently took him to an adjacent room where he sat and allowed the drug cocktail to work its magic on such vital functions like short-term memory, inhibition control, and thought manipulation. Then, She proceeded to indoctrinate him with the story he was to repeat to the authorities when he got caught.

It was a beauty, really, something about the diamond having been handed over to his accomplice who happened to work for the Chinese oil tycoon Lao Ming. The scandal brought about by such accusations would make him lose a lot of money in the stock market and a couple of contracts still waiting to be signed.

As Dean obediently droned the story that was now a part of his true memories, Caldwell sighed as her hands traced every line of his spectacularly addictive body. She really shouldn't indulge in carnal pleasures at that moment but she was sure his unadorned form would make Adonis himself blush and there was something about his lips that made all her senses tingle.

So, without further ado, she listened to the voice of temptation and gave him something else to remember and swallow before she exited the Museum through the front door with the real diamond hidden inside a secret pocket of her suit.

The night air was cool, and fresh, everything that made her tick. Her employer awaited her on a private jet just outside town. In the end, both would get what they wanted.

Funny story, though. When, a couple of days later, the one who hired her services went to the room where he kept his private collection of precious stones from all around the world to look at the Zenobia, all he found was a heavily-secured dome with a large onion inside.

Lesson Number One

Barry struggled against the chains that bound him to the metal chair, to no avail. In fact, the more he tried to fight, the tighter they seemed to get, causing great strain on his wrists and ankles.

"Debra, stop! This is not what I had in mind when I said I wanted to be your slave."

She stopped fiddling with her paraphernalia of kinky toys and looked down at him with a smirk.

"What did you have in mind then?"

"I don't know… something fun, I guess. This isn't fun!" and he shuddered when he saw the jumbo-sized dildo she was holding in her left hand.

Debra smirked again and sat down on his lap. Her latex-clad curves insinuated against his manhood with meticulous care, a relentless tease too strong to be ignored.

"Well, you see… that was your problem from the start. Slavery isn't meant to be fun. It's all about obedience, the recognition of one's natural inferiority towards a superior being. I'm merely giving you what you asked for… you should be thankful!"

"Debra, please…"

"Oh, you'll please, don't worry. There's so much to learn and I'm quite the strict teacher. However, before that, let's make sure you're a bit more… cooperative."

She left the sentence hanging in the air like the sword of Damocles and rose to her feet. Tears rolled down his cheeks as he realized that the proverbial blade was about to hit him hard. He closed his eyes.

They were still closed when he felt a sharp needle pierce his neck and a cold, metal-like liquid invade his bloodstream. The drug spread quickly, triggering burst after burst of dreamy euphoria, and he soon got lost in the mazes of his own mind, a series of interconnected, spiraling hallways with no beginning or end.

After wandering around, confused, for a very long time, he finally saw something different: a small room with a very inviting bed at the center.

As he laid down to rest, a translucent image of Debra appeared between his legs, her ghostly hands wrapped around his shaft. Another reflection knelt by the bed, whispering soft, enticing words about the importance of giving up control and, the two combined, effortlessly, milked his cock and mind.

* * *

In the real world, sitting on a velvet throne a few feet away from him, Debra grinned as she saw him cum. Lesson number one had clearly been a successful one, but there was still a long way to go before his total capitulation to her whims.

One thing was for sure: she was going to enjoy every single moment.

Lesson Number Two

Barry woke up in a daze, eyes slightly defocused, balls aching. What a strange dream!, he thought, reminiscing about Debra's mind-controlling ways. Sexy for sure, yet a dream nonetheless for there was no way an uptight catholic young woman could turn out to be the embodiment of such dark fantasies. He remembered the feeling of helplessly cumming for her over and over again and blushed from head to toe, a sheepish smile in perfect sync with the afterglow in his heart and mind.

All of these pleasant feelings were replaced by utter shock when he saw Dave sitting in a corner of the bedroom. He had been his best friend since times immemorial, a ginger-bearded Baseball fanatic who dreamed of swinging his bat every day of the week, but always failing to get some action. Why was he sitting there when he hadn't been invited in the first place and what was he holding on his left hand?

"Rise and shine, sleepyhead." He smiled.

"What are you doing here?" Barry asked, covering his manhood.

"You asked me to come… and bring you this…" he pointed at the large rubber object in his possession. It looked like… "I always do what you ask."

"Huh? I don't remember any of that," Barry mumbled. "And why the fuck would I ask you to bring me a big, black cock?"

"Because you like cock? Because you crave cock? I don't know. I only did what you told me to do. I always do what you tell me to do."

"You're freaking me out, Dave."

His friend jumped from his seat and on to the king-sized bed, the sinful phallus calling out like a siren from ancient myths.

"Can a freak really be freaked out? You're such a freak, aren't you, Barry? Calling me in the middle of the night to bring you this and then pretending you don't want to play any more? Hmmm… that's what I love about you. You're a real freak with quite the dirty mind. I didn't want to do this but you insisted and when you insist, there's nothing I can do to resist," Dave rubbed the cock on Barry's torso. "I can never resist you, just like you can't resist me, can you? Say it, Barry, say you can't resist…"

"I…" he gulped.

"Fuck me, Dave. Fuck me real bad right now. Say it."

"Hmmm…"

"Fuck me with that big, black cock of yours until I pass out."

"No!"

"You can't help yourself, the fucking has already started. You're fucked time and time again… you'll always be fucked when I'm around."

"Dave, stop!"

"That's not my real name, is it?" He said as he thrusted the dildo inside his half-open mouth.

Barry woke up in a daze, eyes slightly defocused, balls aching, mouth numb, butt cheeks red and sore. What a strange dream!, he thought. Dave was Debra, Debra was Dave but there was no way an uptight catholic young woman could turn out to be the embodiment of such dark fantasies. He remembered the feeling of sinking before her hypnotic might and blushed from head to toe, a sheepish smile in perfect sync with the afterglow in his heart and mind.

"It's time to go back to sleep, now," Debra whispered, and so he did. A bit of confusion and anal play keeps the conscious mind at bay. Lesson number two was complete.

Lovely Day

It was a lovely day at Barnes & Bastion. Karen walked by Brad's cubicle and winked.

"I love you!" He exclaimed.

"I know..." the six-feet tall blue-eyed redhead grinned, continuing down the hallway.

A few meters ahead, she saw Avery taking copies of heart-shaped postcards. His tie got stuck in the copying machine the moment he saw her heavenly face.

"I love you!" He chirped.

"Of course you do..." She patted him in the head before strolling away.

When she reached the coffee room to get her morning latte, twelve kneeling executives had twelve identical offerings in their shaky, grateful hands.

"We love you!" They said in unison.

"And you always will..." she smirked, choosing one of the cups at random and ignoring all the others.

It was a lovely day at Barnes & Bastion, soon to be renamed Karen Rules. She had always dreamed of having her own law firm. The army of lovesick worker drones was just a bonus she would never get tired of. The drugged chocolates she had offered everyone the day before had proven to be a sound investment, one she would repeat in weeks to come. For now, all she wanted was to ditch the stilettos and get a good foot massage.

The moment she reached her new executive office, she buzzed the intercom and asked:

"Which one of you is eager to worship your Goddess?"

The human stampede made the building shake.

Old New

Stephanie Brown finished her interview presentation and contained a sigh of disappointment. Though she had tried her best to impress the leadership present in the room, her most pessimistic side insisted on the notion that she would fail to get the job she had applied for, and she just couldn't stand seeing so much effort go to waste.

Melissa Meyers, Vice-President of Human Resources of the notoriously famous Maxwell Corporation didn't even bother to look up when she finished talking, which convinced her even further that the whole operation had been a major fiasco. She kept on looking at a sheet of yellow paper from behind her turtle shell-rimmed glasses and scribbling notes that no one could understand, except her. Her handwriting was so garbled and strange that some whispered she was better off as a doctor than a businesswoman, and perhaps they were right.

Nonetheless, her silence and apparent disdain for what had just transpired were not to be understood as a flat-out denial of Stephanie's skills, much to the contrary. If she didn't acknowledge her right away, was because she was deeply absorbed in connecting all the dots of her work, making sure that everything had indeed been as appealing as her ears had initially led her to believe. Meyers liked to ponder things to the full extent of her rationality, and was usually pinpoint accurate in selecting the best candidates for the various job requirements.

When she finally finished her mental processes and looked straight into her eyes, a spark of hope was swiftly brought forth.

"That was impressive, really! It seems you did your homework before coming here, Stephanie – may I call you that? – That's a rare thing these days, and I'm a woman that loves dedication! I congratulate you on a job well done!" She exclaimed, before applauding her quite effusively.

"D-does that mean that…" Stephanie gasped. The betrayal of her true emotions was so strong she couldn't even finish the sentence.

"Well, you certainly seem to have the knowledge and expertise it takes to be a valuable asset for this corporation. Nonetheless, before we make things final, there are some wrinkles that need to be ironed out."

"I'm sorry… wrinkles?" Stephanie asked, unsure if she was trying to make a witty remark about her age or meant something else entirely.

"We have high standards here when it comes to our employees. Even those that are approved in the interview selection process with flying colors such as you need to go through one final test before they're finally acknowledged as part of the workforce."

"What kind of test?"

"If you follow me this instant," She said, getting up from his chair. "You'll soon find out, Stephanie."

They left the interview room and proceeded down the very same corridor she had walked through less than an hour before, passing by the crystal desk where a beautiful and elegant young blonde secretary was busy typing something on her touchscreen keyboard. Stephanie loved her purple, classy outfit, but what impressed her the most were the stylish silver headphones with a wireless microphone that, on occasions, seemed to glimmer from within with a powerfully addictive light.

After traversing the main hallway, Meyers eventually turned right and led her to the VIP elevator. Ten floors below them, the Medical Department awaited in all of its technologically sterilized glory, a true testament to the amount of money handled by the corporation on a daily basis.

Stephanie saw state-of-the-art medical equipment, some of which she didn't know to exist for real, and countless men and women wearing shiny lab coats and similar headpieces that gave her the impression she was aboard an interstellar battleship instead of inside the main facilities of a software and hardware company.

Their walk stopped in front of an egg-shaped small chamber or pod connected to a wide multitude of electronic arrays and three-dimensional screens. A doctor of European ascent called Karla Schmidt then explained what was expected of her:

"We've simplified the process of physical and psychological check-up that's mandatory according to state law. This machine will perform a full scan on you that will measure every function of your body and brain to see if they're in accordance with what is considered normal for a woman your age. It takes only a few minutes and the only thing you'll feel is a slight tingle as the optical lasers inside are calibrated. If there are no deviations, no life-endangering conditions found, you're immediately considered fit for duty." The woman smiled.

"And you can start right away if you're up for it!" Meyers concluded, she too quite content.

"Let's do it, then!" Stephanie concurred, more than intrigued by the uncanny apparatus in front of her. Besides, even if she wasn't, knowing that stepping inside the machine was the final threshold before securing a very well-paid job was motivation enough on its own.

The pod was cushioned and quite soft to the touch, and also larger on the inside than what it looked like seen from the exterior. Luminous bulbs were everywhere, some green, some red, some yellow and a couple more that were of an undecided color, seeing they flashed at random intervals through various phases of the common luminous specter. When the door silently slid into place, locking her in, a small rush of claustrophobia assaulted her, yet it was so brief she would never remember it again. Dr. Schmidt's warm voice was heard coming in from a speaker above.

"Initiating scan. Please remain as still as possible for the next five minutes for the data to be properly collected."

Stephanie took a deep breath and did as asked as the lights that surrounded her began to twirl. It appeared that the pod was built onto a rotating axis and was now gently spinning, almost like rocking a baby's cradle. The laser beams followed the same pattern, strangely contorting as they were being fired in rapid succession. There was also something solid about them, an impression of silky wrappings, or maybe something slightly rubbery, she couldn't really tell. It was an odd feeling, for sure, but the tingling was nice, overall. Another sentence echoed in her ears.

"Molecular reversion program in 5, 4, 3, 2..."

"Huh, what?" Stephanie's mind raced as the words gained a dangerous emphasis. The chamber's clockwise rotations intensified, the lights that looked like bindings grew in size, and the world shrunk into an oppressive bubble, practically becoming silvery-white. She was restrained from head to toe, compressed and reshaped like a lump of clay as she felt her clothes shredding, her flesh burning, the laws of Nature being bounced around and ultimately discarded in the trash bin of Science.

The five minutes were, in fact, five hours, and she loved them all, with a perfectly acute awareness. She felt the rejuvenating of the skin, the saggy lumps of flesh becoming firm again, the hair growing stronger and framing the face of a twenty-year-old dazzling woman, the one she remembered being a little over three decades ago. But there was more. She was sculpted, re-sculpted, rearranged over and over until she was the epitome of bodily perfection and a perfect body deserved a perfect mind.

That's what she got when she was freed from the pod and given her very own set of headphones. Irresistible brainwave controllers, they tuned in automatically to the frequencies that made her tick, maintaining all of the attributes she already possessed, yet enhancing them exponentially at the same time. The interface, once fully synchronized, opened her eyes to the reality of being a part of a living intranet, where everyone was always connected, like drones inside a human hive.

Stephanie was now Stephanie, but also Karla, and Bob, and Jo, and endless others, a young and vibrant personification of an ever-growing Collective that would revel in ceaseless manifestations of total conformity.

Her interview presentation had been a smashing hit. She now had a new job, a new family, and a new organic version of an old memory of life. And the best part of it all was when the headphones glimmered, and new streams of data were fed directly to her central nervous system: she was fully upgradeable!

Slavery Night

Archibald McCullough hates Christmas and when I say "hate", I really mean it, in the most visceral way possible. Comparing him to the likes of Ebenezer Scrooge would be easy but also highly inappropriate, because Scrooge was just a character and he's the real deal.

To uncover the real reasons for such an aversion would be a massive undertaking and also a low blow to the Holiday Spirit so I'm not going to bother. I'll say this though: try to talk to him about anything Christmas-related and you're likely to get a shiner as a present.

The thing that really gets on his nerves though are the carols, the syrupy lyrics echoed by smiling faces, and the constant ringing of the bells lambasting his brain. Can you hear that appalling scream being carried in the wind right now? That's him, cursing the world at every possible turn whenever Christmas draws near.

Now, given this opening and all, you're probably wondering why you're reading this, right? Boring, give us the juicy bits already, you're saying. Well then, I will, because juicy stuff is my game anyway, and some pieces of information are too good to be kept hidden for long.

So, like I said, Archibald – let's just call him "Archie" from now on – hates Christmas, right? Wrong, I was just messing with you all. In truth, the correct tense is hated, obviously, because he met me at the mall, yesterday morning.

I'm not sure if he bumped into me or if I bumped into him, it doesn't really matter whatever the case. All I know is that he gave me the most ferocious of looks upon noticing I was humming Silent Night.

"Don't you just love this time of the year?" I asked, batting my long eyelashes at him as I picked up my bags.

"Bah, what's there to love?" He spat.

"Why, everything of course! The lights, the food, the joy in the air... I love Christmas! If I could have it every single day, I'd be a very happy woman!"

"Blatant hypocrisy all year long? No, thank you!"

"That's not a very nice thing to say."

"I don't care. Now, if you'll excuse me..."

And then, just like that, he pushed me. Yes, you've read it correctly, but let me spell it out nonetheless... P-U-S-H-E-D me, and I'm not the kind of the woman to sit idly in the face of such disrespectful behavior. I mean, if you were in my shoes, would you?

As he was leaving, I picked up my smartphone, managed to get a clear picture of him as he negotiated a pathway towards the nearest escalator and all sorts of preparations came to mind just like that. Yes, I love Christmas, but I love the rush of uncovering secrets even more.

What I found out in my explorations wasn't pretty. Archie really had a tendency for violence. Now, as the late Jim Morrison once said, Violence isn't always evil. What's evil is the infatuation with violence, but he sure enjoyed flirting with danger. Newspaper clippings and police reports from the last decade painted the picture of a man who was a borderline sociopath, and I'm a peace lover by heart so, naturally, I had to do something.

If you're familiar with my style already, then you know how persuasive I can be, right? I really am a good teacher, and would have fitted in any given classroom in the world if I wanted to. After careful consideration, I went for something I never tried before. Ladies and gentlemen, welcome to Christmas Ornament Swinging 101!

Imagine a ball, any color you like. Green, perhaps. Or purple. Or blue. Now, imagine Archie answering the door with the same angry eyes he exhibited when we first met. Can you picture his frustration, his haphazard attempts to comprehend how I managed to find out where he lived and know pretty much everything about him in just a couple of hours? Can you see his lips curling outward in a pathetic attempt at a growl as I kicked him in the nuts and had him stare at the beautiful swinging motions? If you can visualize all that, including the soft reflections slowly rendering his pupils still, perhaps you should stop reading for a bit, take a breather, and come back after a while, okay?

Oh, you don't want that? My, my… are you going to tell me all your kinky fantasies, too?

Anyway, Archie stopped protesting soon enough just like I hoped he would, and then we moved on to what's really important.

Christmas is a time of happiness, communion, celebration. To me, singing from the top of our lungs is a pleasure like no other so, of course, I taught him something new, and will keep on doing so until the year is done. Remember Silent Night? Beautiful song for sure, but this one's better. Go on, Archie boy, what are you waiting for?

"Yes, Mistress. Hmmm…

Slavery night, blissful night,

All thoughts fade in the light

Will is boring, an endless chore

Strip it all right into the core

So I can really be free

So I can really be free…

Slavery night, blissful night,

Trance is good, feels so right

Only Your words are real to me

Forever obedient I wish to be
Kneeling even when standing
Kneeling even when standing…

Slavery night, blissful night
Eyes upon You, glorious sight
By the fire, with a collar at hand
I await the supreme command:
" 'round your neck, pet of mine
'round your neck, pet of mine…"

The Horror of Brunwyn

One of the maxims that survived the First Era of Careth goes like this: If you go walking through the Woods of Brunwyn and the silver owls with human-like voices begin whispering, run because Death is approaching fast!

Throughout the ages, many were the unwary that failed to listen to such warnings, and none of them lived for long after the furry horror ambushed them. It is said that the owls can mimic the appalling screams of the agonizing victims if they so wish, but listening to them is pretty much a death sentence as well, for they draw out the beast from its hiding place, deep within the mass of perennial trees with dark-red leaves.

Lydian of Smividell, High Priestess of the Temple of Yandinn located within the West Section of the Diamond City of Annazeth, was no fool and walked through the Woods with purpose. The one she served with all her heart was The Goddess of the Forest and had spoken to her through the vibrant flowers that grew in the Temple Gardens. The message had been clear: it was time to quell the mythical beast and no one could do it, except her.

This formidable task would have most people run away in fear, but she was a woman of unshakable faith, and nothing discouraged her. She pressed forward in her rainbow-colored gown, and wearing proudly the golden diadem of her status, listening to the sounds of the owls with utmost care. The moment they gave the warning, she would have to prepare herself.

The first whispers came quickly, perhaps quicker than she had anticipated. Though the owls were everywhere in the branches above her, Lydian couldn't see them unless they wanted to be seen. The way they mumbled, the sound propagating from left to right, gave her a direction to be attentive to. Raising her hands to the air, she began chanting.

It jumped from an unknown place and landed less than ten feet away from her. The beast was over eight feet tall and, despite some humanoid traits, it resembled a hideous combination of wolf and ape, with a pig snout thrown in the mix. It had big, black eyes and two sets of retractable, sharp claws that could rip apart any living creature that stood in its way. Lydian saw the monstrosity, yet did not shiver. Instead, she kept humming the secret incantation she had been revealed, hoping for its effects to manifest.

The air around her grew heavier as if gravity itself was suffering the effects of the arcane magic being unleashed. When the beast charged furiously, it clashed against an invisible barrier and fell to the floor, gasping for air. Lydian spread out her palms and fired two darts of pure thought energy straight into its brain.

The creature growled as it felt the intruding thoughts, its enormous body arching, unnaturally. Lydian kept on pressing forward in her subduing intentions, exploring each psychic connection as it appeared before her mind's eye and couldn't help but feel intrigued by what she eventually found.

She sensed the remnants of a spell there, a form of familiar magic that had certainly been more powerful in bygone years, but one that still survived in an almost parasitical fashion, feeding off the strength of the creature and keeping it imprisoned. Focusing all her energy, she visualized the mystic binding as a series of threads first and then gave it the shape of a luminous snake which she then proceeded to crush.

The horror of Brunwyn laid his massive head back and this time, it screamed as the nefarious influence that had kept it restrained for so long, erupted from its mouth in a cascade of wriggling light. As it fell to the ground and disappeared, the monster's shape began to change.

The silent owls and the stunned High Priestess watched as muscles and skin contracted, and the animal's size was cut in half; they saw the claws receding into hands and all the fur fall down, and the hideous visage become the one of a beautiful dark-haired woman with purple eyes and equally purple luscious lips. She wore a dazzling silver and black armor forged in the fiery pits surrounding the city of Son-Dhár to the east and held a dark sword with dozens of tiny crystals embedded on the blade whose color seemed to be blood red.

Lydian had seen numerous drawings and references in forbidden tomes to know exactly who this mysterious woman was, but she was shocked nonetheless. How could a General of the Ancients be alive after so many years and why, oh why had she released it from its magical curse? Yandinn surely knew what the creature really was, and yet she had ordered her to quell it, fully knowing she would find the spell and break it in the process... it made no sense!

"You are..." She muttered, having a hard time combining words into a proper sentence.

"Rakhael, Emissary of the Ancient's will, O High Priestess of Yandinn." the woman answered as she rose to her feet and smiled, diabolically. "I have to thank you for the kindness of setting me free from that horrible shape one of your predecessors imposed upon me near the end of The First Era." Her sword glimmered. "Only someone trained in the same ways could break it and you did so admirably."

"What's the meaning of this? Yandinn and The Ancients are sworn enemies since always. Why did...?"

Rakhael brandished her sword in a strangely, voluptuous way. If was as if the blade was dancing in-between her fingers. The crystals started glowing.

"Hmmm... your Goddess spoke to you, did she? Are you sure about that? Even when my spirit was sealed in that grotesque form, I could feel that Careth is changing again, that the old is coming back to claim the new. Don't you know that Zarn'Gha already walks among us? She is getting stronger with each passing second, you see? I bet she is already powerful enough to deceive a gullible person such as you..."

"That is a lie!" Lydian shouted and focused all of her power to bring forth a deadly beam of magic.

Rakhael saw it coming and remained still as the hoary armor absorbed the discharge quite effortlessly. Her sword kept twirling, the crystal's radiance intensifying. Above them, a thousand invisible wings flapped away.

"The only lie here is the one you believe in. You have been played the fool, High Priestess, by forces that longed for my return, in the same way I longed for theirs! Zarn'Gha will be pleased with her new toy."

The sword stopped spinning and Rakhael's lips uttered a single word in the language only those that directly served the Ancients knew. One by one, the crystals detached themselves from the blade and flew towards Lydian who had no time to muster a reaction whatsoever. They pierced her dress and latched onto her pale skin in the arms, legs, neck, and forehead, branding her with strings of suggestions that made her weak and compliant. It was not a power as strong as the Bliss of Zarn'Gha, but it was solid enough to ensure that the High Priestess would not try anything foolish until she was delivered as a present, and had her mind defiled once and for all. Tears wanted to roll down Lydian's glassy eyes, but they were not allowed to. Any willful action or thought had lost its meaning.

Rakhael leaned towards her and kissed her avidly on the lips, just a taste of the ecstatic rush she had missed during her spellbinding captivity. The Horror of Brunwyn was no more but new manifestations of dread would rise, now that she was free to continue her work as Emissary and General of The Ancients. Yes, Careth was definitely changing and the silver owls with human-like voices were sure to have many sad songs to sing in the dark times ahead.

The Pet's Reward

Francine turned on the basement lights and approached the small cage. Stretching a booted foot, she demanded the compliance of the animal locked within. The dog formerly known as Kyle pushed its tongue through the bars and eagerly licked the tip of her footwear ever so grateful for the divine treat.

"Did you sleep well last night?" She asked. "No more nightmares, I hope."

Although it still understood her words, Dog-Kyle could no longer articulate them in response. Instead, it let out a small whimper of approval. The strange visions where it had two legs to walk upright instead of four beautiful furry paws had indeed faded and if they should ever return, its Owner would take care of them once more. She always did for she was powerful enough to fend off ill thoughts. Dog-Kyle loved her very much. Dog-Kyle was completely loyal and subservient to her.

"Can you believe it's been a year already?" She offered him the other leather boot. "That Valentine's when we met was the best of my life. This one will be the best of yours."

Oh, God! Yes! Yes! Yes! It was getting out! Owner was giving it a chance to crawl at her feet again. Dog-Kyle let out a joyful howl as she laughed but the best news were yet to come.

The second cage arrived during the afternoon, its new companion a couple of hours later. Its smell was familiar somehow, but any traces of recognition were wiped clean from its mind the moment their eyes crossed. Dog-Kyle would never be allowed to remember his older brother again.

You Never…

Jeremy looked at the chastity cage Gretchen was holding and then into her beautiful, sparkly brown eyes. Her conditioning was strong but not so strong that prevented him from talking. The daze in his thoughts cleared away long enough for him to articulate a sentence before coming back in full strength, a honeyed trap impossible to forget.

"I'm not wearing that…" he muttered.

"Of course you're not, my dear," she assured him with a mischievous smile. "You never do anything I ask you to do when you look into my eyes because when you look into my eyes you know that I don't even need asking. If I asked, I would be upset for having to do so and, although you would be compelled to obey, knowing I'm upset would make you feel bad about yourself. You don't want me to be upset and therefore you don't want me to ask and, since I'm not asking, you'll do it willingly to make sure I don't ever have to ask again, won't you? In fact, you're the one that's going to be asking me something very soon. What is it you want to ask me, pet?"

"May I please wear that?" he drooled, the happiness of his girlfriend and Mistress quieting the confusion of his thoughts.

"Took you long enough…" She grinned.

Vampires

Hello. Today, I would like to talk to you about vampires, those fascinating creatures that seem to be all the rage once again.

These supernatural predators have manifested themselves throughout History in many forms. Of course, the most famous are the blood-sucking type because of all the lore and literature written about them. They're usually portrayed as diabolical beings although, in recent times, many efforts have been made to humanize them a little, make them less scary and somewhat more alluring in the process but I prefer the classic tales myself - they simply had more charm to them!

But there are also other kinds of vampires that people usually don't talk about, for instance, those that feed exclusively off the fluids of sexual rapture. They like to stalk young couples, drawn by their pheromones and lust, lurking in the shadows until the moment is ready to strike. They're quite vicious but their numbers have dwindled considerably so, most likely, you'll never have to worry about being attacked by one.

I could go on babbling forever about all the species and sub-species, but I'll speak only of one other type, my favorite of them all.

These vampires have none of the traits and weaknesses usually associated with the word. They don't have fangs, don't turn into bats or smoke, and certainly aren't afraid of the sun! They're regular people in every aspect except one. They can attack from a distance and they slowly take control of their preys by absorbing the mental energy required for simple, innocent tasks like clicking a mouse button or taking the time to read a short story such as this one.

Thanks for the meal.

About the author

S.B., Simple Being, middle name Creative. Writer and artist with a penchant for themes of Femdom Hypnosis and Mind Control. His thoughts are his own except when they're not.

Besides indulging himself in kinky delights, he loves his furry family of two (dogs), sci-fi and horror stories, and puns galore. He's also been writing a piece of erotic micro-fiction every single day since January 1st, 2016 and has no intention of stopping anytime soon.

Find out more and keep up with his latest extravaganzas by visiting and supporting his personal website, Spell... B-O-U-N-D.